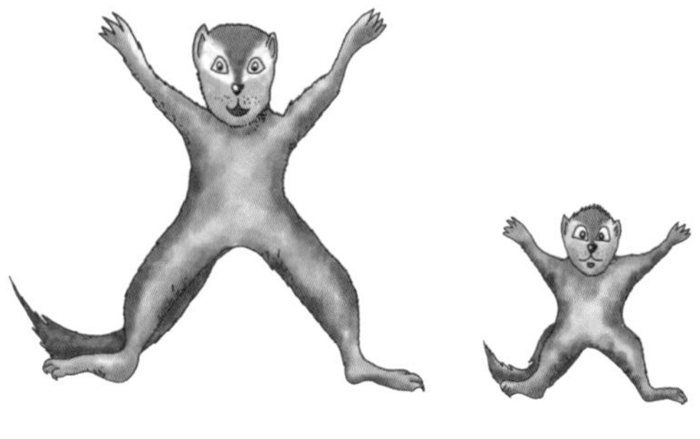

Animalphabetical Adventures

Publication: January 2020

Published in Canada by
Bayeux Arts Digital - Traditional Publishing
2403, 510 6th Avenue, S.E.
Calgary, Canada T2G 1L7

www.bayeux.com

Cover design by Kinga White
Book design by Kinga White

Library and Archives Canada Cataloguing in Publication

Title: Animalphabetical Adventures / Kinga White.
Names: White, Kinga, author, illustrator.
Identifiers: Canadiana (print) 20190153288 | Canadiana (ebook) 20190153334 | ISBN 9781988440316 (hardcover) | ISBN 9781988440323 (HTML)
Subjects: LCSH: English language — Alphabet — Juvenile literature. | LCSH: Animals — Juvenile literature.
Classification: LCC PE1155 .W55 2019 | DDC j421/.1—dc23

The ongoing publishing activities of Bayeux Arts Digital - Traditional Publishing under its varied imprints are supported by the Government of Alberta, Alberta Multimedia Development Fund, and the Government of Canada through the Book Publishing Industry Development Program.

Kinga White

Animalphabetical Adventures

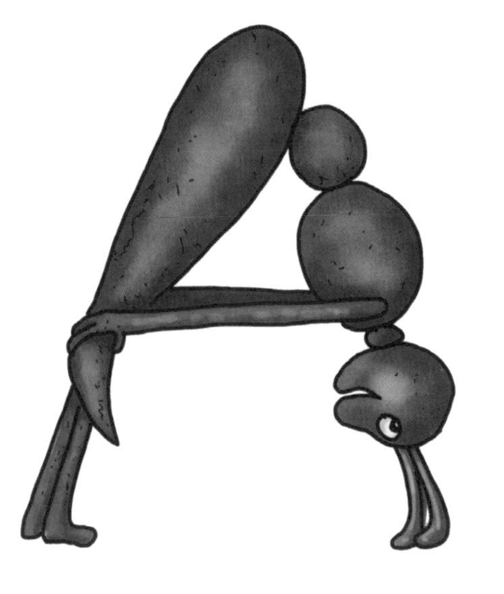

Suddenly, a large swirly tunnel dropped in the soil;
It looked so inviting the ant stopped her toil.

Intrigued, the ant climbed inside the corridor,
To find where it led, and explore a little more.

The tunnel was moist
with wind blowing in and out.

Ant

A busy little ant was moving
soil for a mound,
When she felt the ground shake
and heard a sniffing sound.

Oh no! It was the inside of an aardvark's snout!

The ant knew
she had climbed
into his long nose
And tickled him
by moving her
teeny little toes.

The aardvark begged the little ant to come out quickly.
As her going up and down was terribly tickly.

But the ant could not hear inside his long nose
And she found it quite exciting to swirl on her toes.

The tickling was too much,
it made the aardvark sneeze
And the ant flew out of his nose
in a **strong wheeze**.

Bear

A big brown bear walked
through the dense wood;
With his tummy rumbling
as he looked for some food.

The sweet scent of honey
had drawn him to a tree,
So he climbed way up high
to the open cavity.

The curious bear
put his hairy paw
inside the sticky trunk
And started scooping
honeycomb chunk after chunk.

The honey was so delicious
he could not resist;
He didn't see all the bees
gathering on his fist.

When he took his paw out,
it was full of angry bees.
They all thundered:

'Stay away from our honey, please!'

Then hundreds and hundreds
flew out of the busy nest
Surrounding the bear,
pulling fur and lifting his chest.

'If you EVER come back
to our home, our tree,
We will sting you till you cry!'
said the chief bee.

With fearsome force the bear was raised right up to the sky
And flown out of the forest in the blink of an eye.

Just under water with only
his eyes poking out
Floated a lazy crocodile
with a shiny snout.

Crocodile

Deep in Africa a river
cut through the hard sand
Bringing needed refreshment
to the dry land.

Giraffes and a rhino stood
by the bank in scorching heat;
Dreaming of cooling down,
not daring to dip their feet.

There was someone
in the river who made
their hearts pound,
So they decided to stay
on the burning hot ground.

The croc roared:
**"Hey guys!?
Why don't you join
me to cool down?"**

But the tempted giraffes
said **"No!"**
with a fearful frown.

Nowhere in sight was
a tree, bush or even
long grass.
The croc thought
they couldn't wait for
the heatwave to pass.

Suddenly he had an idea
and he yelled,
**"Only one thing
can be done!"**

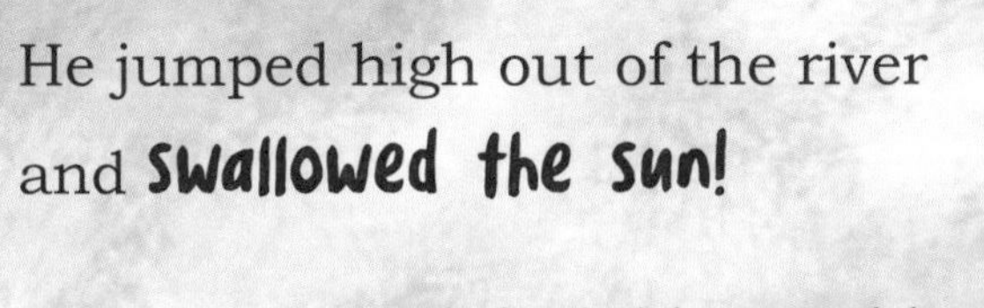

He jumped high out of the river
and **swallowed the sun!**

The sky turned dark blue and looked not so bright;
It felt pleasantly cool, like in the dead of night.

All the animals there stared in complete disbelief
When just like that the crocodile had become a thief!

They were thankful for the crocodile's assistance
And felt sheepish about their initial resistance.

Duck

A lone duck was rushing
to escape the biting cold,
As the frost rolled in,
calling winter to unfold.

The duck was trying to pack
and leave as the last one,
While her family waited
for her in the sun.

She grabbed her stuff
and started on a long
flight down south,
When on her way
she tasted a rain drop
in her mouth.

The darkening skies
opened up
to a dreadful storm
And dozens of thick,
fast-moving clouds
began to form.

The frightened duck
flew as fast as she could
with closed eyes
So as not to look
at the storm
ripping through
the skies.

Not knowing where she was going
the duck lost control;
Then got tangled up in something
and began to roll.

When the cold rain stopped,
the bird felt a sunny fleck.
**That's when she saw a rainbow
wrapped around her neck!**

It fluttered gracefully
as the duck was falling down,
Watching the strip of coloured light
with a puzzled frown.

The duck found her balance back
as the sky was clearing
And saw her family looking up cheering.

Elephant

As the lazy sun was settling in
for a good night's sleep
A howling wind rushed in
with a powerful sweep.

The air filled with baobab leaves
swirling all around
And dry savannah grass
made an eerie hissing sound.

A baby elephant got
caught up in this storm,
He held onto a tree
but his trunk got almost torn.

When he peered around
into the dark blue sky,
He noticed a snake and
a zebra flying way up high.

As the minutes passed
the gale grew stronger
And the small elephant
couldn't hold any longer.

So he let go
and was blown away
very, very far.
When he opened his eyes,
he was lying on a star.

frog

In the autumn afternoon
right next to a big pond
Sat a frog waving a straw,
pretending it's a wand.

Swirling it left and right,
then pointing the straw up high;
Blowing bubbles,
watching them drift
into the blue sky.

Just when the frog was blowing
his biggest bubble yet,
The sky turned a strange yellow
and a howling wind set.

It swept the frightened frog
right off the ground,

Lifting colourful leaves,
making a loud rattling
sound.

As the frog was drifting
further and further away,
Two hedgehogs,
who were passing by,
looked up in dismay.

At once they came up
with a smart and cunning plan.
One of them pulled out
a long quill from
his back and ran.

When at full speed,
he threw the arrow
with all his might,
Bursting the bubble
so the frog began
to lose height.

Sailing through the yellow sky
with the broadest smile,
The lucky frog fell gently
on the dry leaves' pile.

Gorilla

On an endless desert filled
with sparkling golden sand
The sun rose above the dunes
and sunshine bathed the land.

The sky turned to pastel shades
of purple and red,
When a tired round moon
got ready for bed.

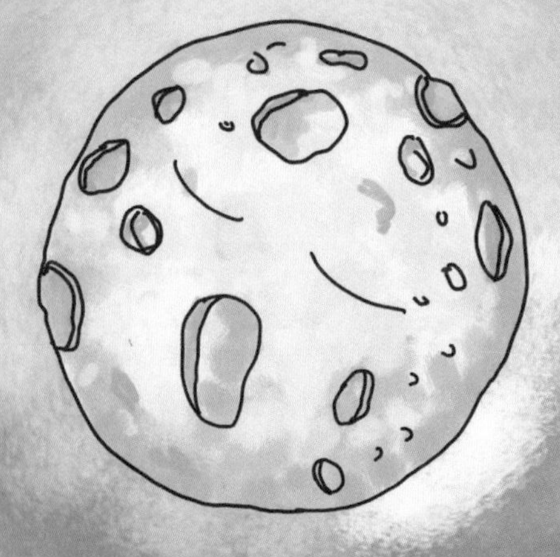

Moving in the distance one could see a black dot
That, when closer, got bigger and easier to spot.

A large hairy creature appeared between the dunes
Filling the air with sounds of humming, cheerful tunes.

It was a huge gorilla,
travelling through the night;
He was so hungry he could
really do with a bite.

But the desert was nothing but heaps of endless sand,
Where not a single fruit tree could ever stand.

The gorilla stuck his head through the clouds up high
And saw a **glorious round piece of cheese** in the sky.

Looking at this inviting treat he started to drool;
So he grabbed the moon right away and bit off a mouthful.

Horse

At the bottom of a mountain range
there lived a blonde horse
Whose snooty attitude
could not have been worse.

One frosty morning
trotting past a bighorn sheep,
He said, "I have sleek, long hair
and my eyes are so deep".

Then off he proudly went with his head up high,
When a young skunk eating a honeybee caught his eye.

Look at me he said, "I have beautiful shiny hair,
I never get frightened and I don't stink up the air!"

Off he went prancing
on the frozen solid ground,
When he heard a mountain
lion make a purring sound.

The horse said,
**"I am so fit and
I can even climb a tree".**
So he clambered on a branch
for everyone to see.

But how to get down
from up high, this
the horse didn't know.
He held on to the branch
and screamed for help
from below.

So the bighorn sheep stood
rigid under the tree trunk,
A squirrel clambered on,
then the lion,
then the skunk.

They all formed a ladder
for the horse to come down,
Who turned red
from embarrassment
and felt like a **clown**.

A crowd of keen bugs
gathered by the starting line;
Chatting loud, impatiently
waiting for a sign.

Insect

In tall grass insects lived
in a large community.
They were most active
and loved living in unity.

They built towers together
and hunted for food;
They enjoyed having company,
it made them feel good.

One day the insect elders
organised a big race;
Critters from surrounding
grasslands came over to chase.

The head judge said,
"Ready, set, go!"
shaking the chime,
But a beetle seemed to
have got stuck in gooey slime!

"Please wait!"
he cried in despair,
"I want to take part too!"
A grasshopper jumped to pull him
out off the greenish goo.

He pulled with all his strength
on the beetle's hard horn,
But the beetle shouted "**OUCH!**"
as it was getting torn.

With a bang and a splash
they were freed from the slime
And somehow landed right
next to the finish line!

Jellyfish

On top of a lofty
coastal cliff, facing west,
Rested the spotty egg
of a seagull in a nest.

Suddenly, a gust of wind
lifted the egg up high
And dropped it in the ocean
catching the seagull's eye.

Frantic, she hovered
over the waters so blue,
But where to begin looking,
she had no clue.

Then a glassy jellyfish
came swimming by,
Who offered to help,
hearing the seagull's cry.

The jellyfish dived
straight under and
began the search.
She couldn't see well
as the sudden waves
made her lurch.

So she went deep
past coral reefs and
a school of fish,
Who gracefully moved
their colourful tails
with a swish.

The deeper the jellyfish went,
the darker it got;
Until not even
a glimpse of sunlight
could be caught.

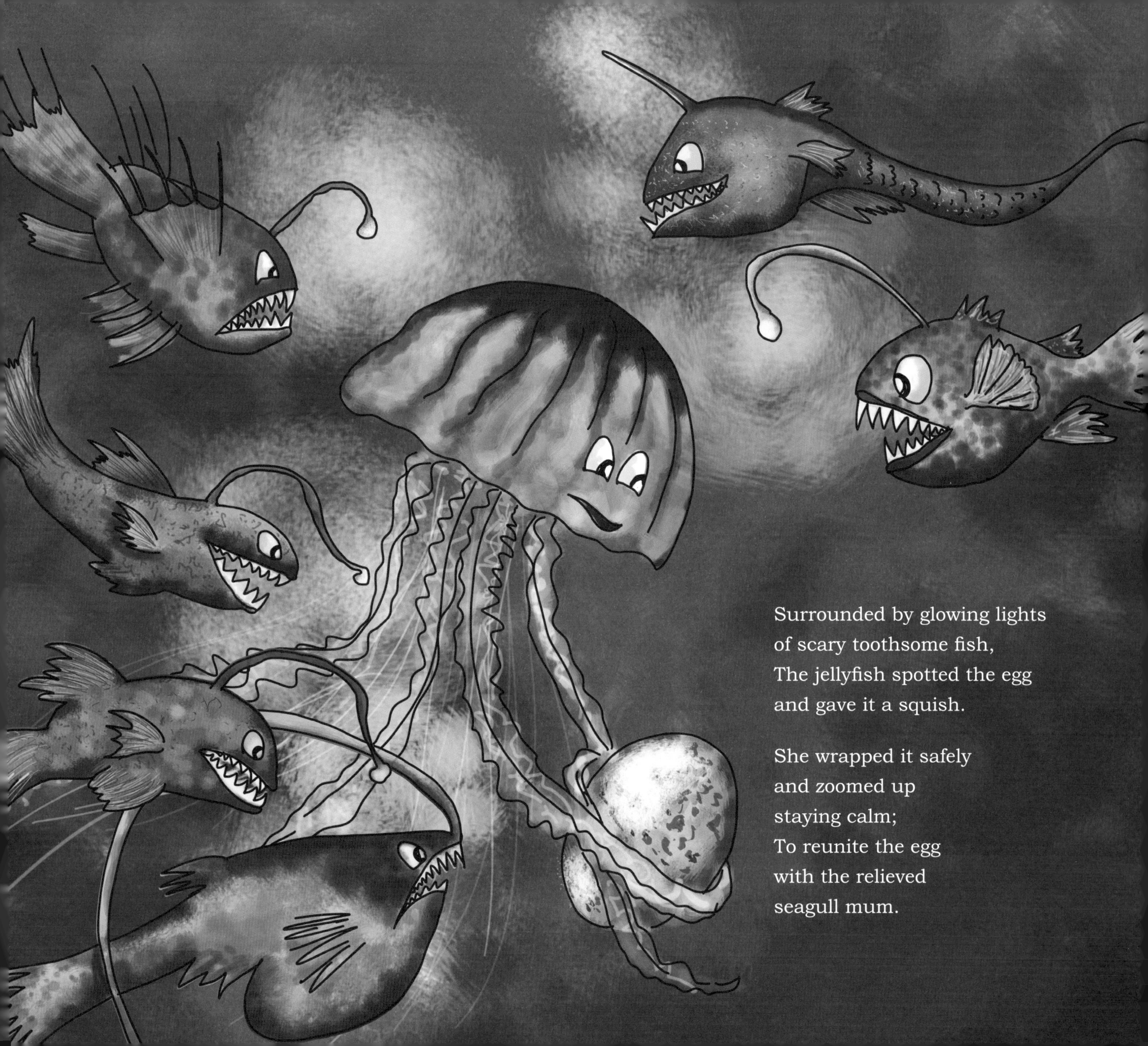

Surrounded by glowing lights
of scary toothsome fish,
The jellyfish spotted the egg
and gave it a squish.

She wrapped it safely
and zoomed up
staying calm;
To reunite the egg
with the relieved
seagull mum.

Leaves to the left, leaves to the right,
leaves above her head;
She even used one large juicy leaf as her bed.

Exhausted and unwell she wanted to feel free
And get to see places away from the leafy tree.

One night dozens of glowing lights lit up the sky;
It was a swarm of fireflies who were flying by.

Koala

High up in the crown
of a eucalyptus tree
Sat an ageing koala
who wanted to feel free.

All her life she lived
in the canopied tree up high,
With thousands of dark green
eucalyptus leaves nearby.

The koala's desire to follow
was so strong
That she just rose above
the trees without waiting long.

Blown by a gust of wind
she flew into the night,
Enchanted by the fireflies'
mesmerizing light.

As she looked down
at a world of many hues,
The koala marvelled
at the breathtaking views.

Her heart filled with joy
and her body became light;
She landed on a star to rest
and held to it tight.

Sitting comfy with crossed legs,
feeling content and free,
The koala looked down
and waved to her family.

To catch some wind,
he tried to run as fast as light,
But, soon out of breath,
his chest felt quite tight.

Lion

In the middle of the
scorching hot African sun
Lay an old majestic lion
not having much fun.

He was really bothered
by his very thick mane,
In the terrible heat
it was driving him insane.

He tried to flatten his hair
by standing on his head,
But when he got up
he felt dizzy instead.

He went off to perch
on a baobab tree up high,
When three colourful sunbirds
happened to fly nearby.

They looked at the lion
and saw his worried frown,
Then grabbed his shaggy hair
and swirled left, right,
up and down.

And just like that with twirls and loops,
they made a thick braid,
Which cooled the lion with his woven mane
in the shade.

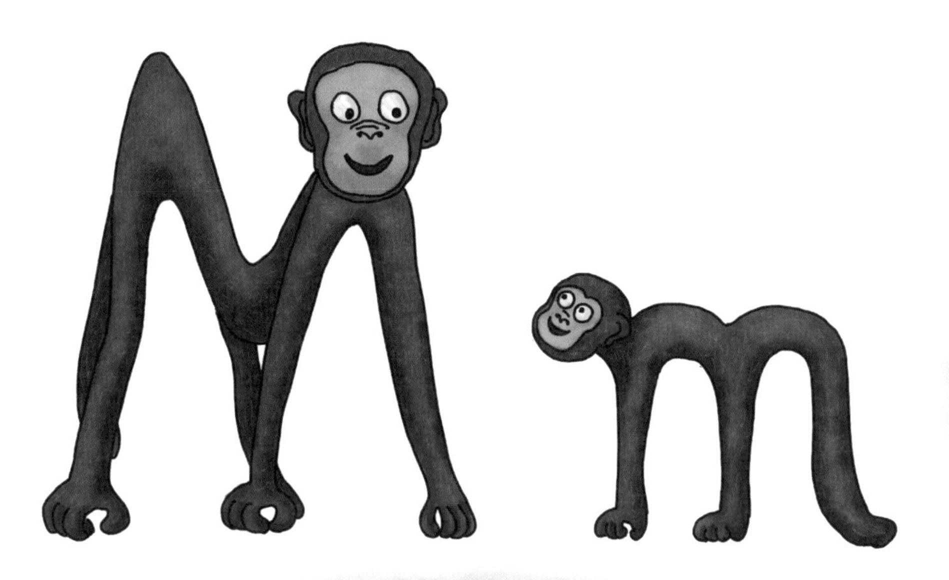

Monkey

A baby monkey lay cuddled up
on a palm tree,
Fighting off sleep whilst
staring at the turquoise sea.

Just then a butterfly flew in
with a petal of a rose
And gently plopped down
on the baby monkey's nose.

"Hold the petal,"
the butterfly said
in a soft whisper
And the monkey glided off
in swirls like a twister.

They both fell down
and landed in a magical place;
The monkey couldn't hide
the excitement on his face.

He lay in tall flowers
bursting with sweet scent
Where his light baby body
hardly made a dent.

Just then the monkey felt
a rather cold water drop;
When he opened his eyes
he was back on the tree top.

He then pointed
his long twisted tusk
towards the sun
And gazed at
the rays reflecting
on it when he spun.

Amazed with
the sun-beams
on his tusk,
he thought out loud:

Narwhal

On a frosty morning
in a picturesque fjord,
A large narwhal swam slowly
feeling terribly bored.

Staring at the palette
of surrounding shades of blue,
Lazily wondering what
he could possibly do.

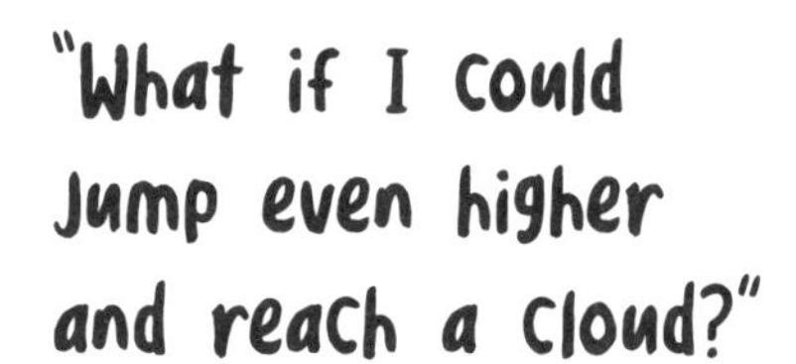

**"What if I could
jump even higher
and reach a cloud?"**

He leaped out of the water
right into the blue sky
And with his tusk, he pierced
a cloud that was flying by.

He then spun it round until it got fluffy and sweet
Creating a rainbow candy floss ready to eat!

Right away, three puffins
were drawn to the sweet scent;
They took big bites of candy floss
leaving a big dent.

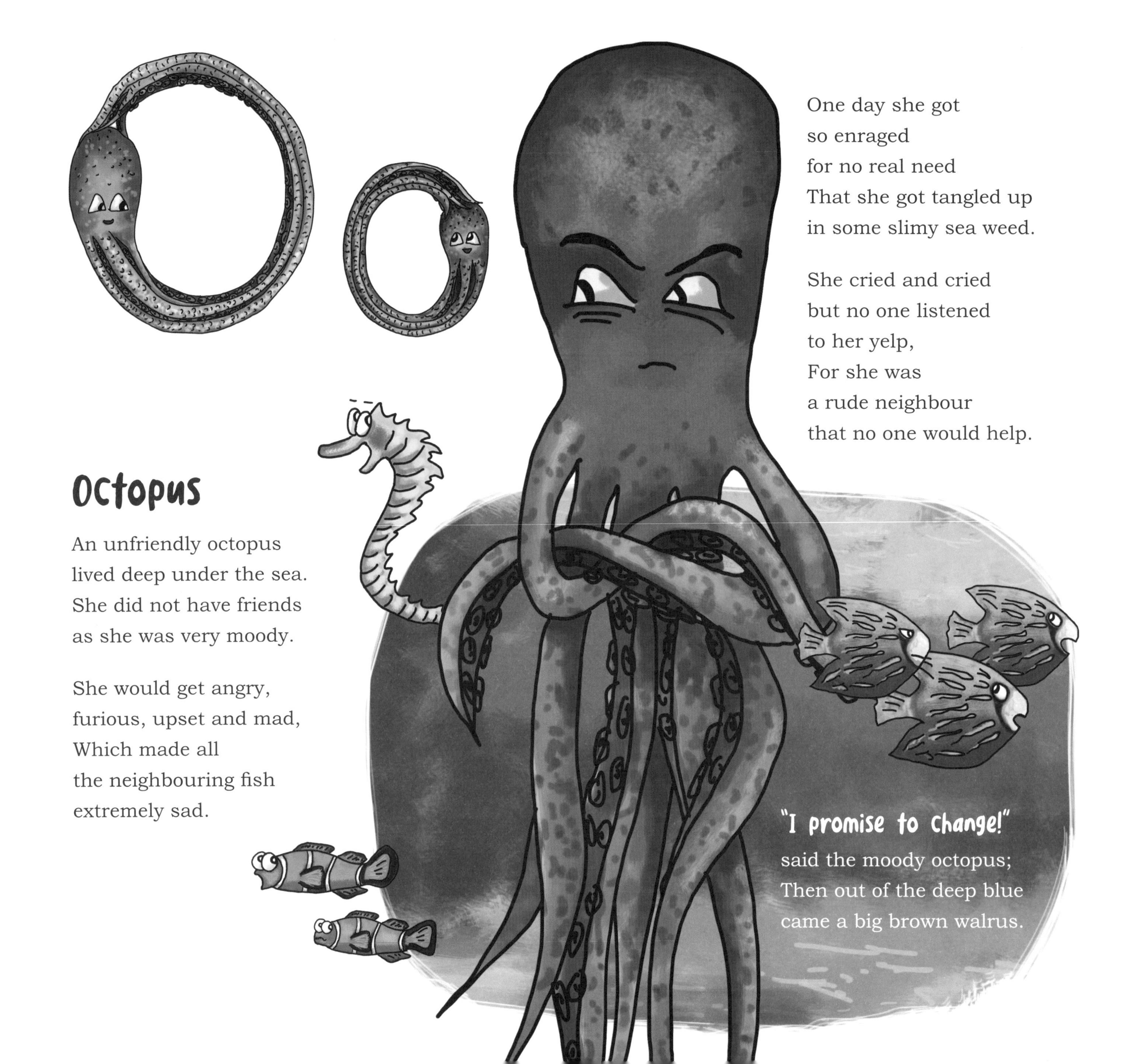

Octopus

An unfriendly octopus
lived deep under the sea.
She did not have friends
as she was very moody.

She would get angry,
furious, upset and mad,
Which made all
the neighbouring fish
extremely sad.

One day she got
so enraged
for no real need
That she got tangled up
in some slimy sea weed.

She cried and cried
but no one listened
to her yelp,
For she was
a rude neighbour
that no one would help.

"I promise to change!"
said the moody octopus;
Then out of the deep blue
came a big brown walrus.

"Your tantrums
got you nowhere
you silly old thing.
Show compassion and
kindness that's what
makes us cling!"

I'll help you this time
as you'd be here till dusk
And I'll cut the tangled seaweed
with my sharp tusk."

Since that day the octopus
was friendly and kind,
With many animals
covering her behind.

Penguin

Way up in the north,
next to the cold Arctic Sea
Amongst tall icebergs
there lived a penguin family.

With a penguin mum,
dad and two little
penguin brothers,
They all stayed in a cold,
draughty home
with no others.

Expecting a new
baby brother any day now,
The penguin mum
wanted to keep
the house warm somehow.

One night the penguin father
came up with a grand plan;
He had an idea how
to bring warmth to his clan.

He climbed all the way up
to the highest iceberg peak

And **Jumped**
onto a cloud
hooking to it
with his beak.

He then cast his fishing rod
into the deep blue sky
And waited patiently for
a bright star to float by.

Suddenly, he felt
the line tighten
with a loud **Zing!**
He pulled in his rod
and squeezed the star
under his wing.

He quickly jumped off the cloud
and ran home with his catch
And made it just in time
for the new penguin to hatch.

Quail

In a glaring hot desert lived
a small brown-grey quail,
Who so badly wanted
to have a colourful tail.

Jealous of other birds
and their beautiful feathers
She went to dye her tail
in the hottest of weathers.

Under a big rock she found
a blueberry bush;
She picked all the berries
and rolled in them in a whoosh.

She rolled and jumped,
but no colour would stick
to her tail;
Desperate, the quail
would do anything not to fail!

She tried rays of sun for red
and cactus skin for green,
Moonlight to make it white,
but no colour could be seen.

Out of nowhere a big, hungry jackal
strolled around
Wondering where a tasty treat
for dinner could be found.

The frightened quail sat between
the dry bush and a rock
Hoping the jackal wouldn't notice her
and continue his walk.

The bird could not be seen
so the jackal went away
**And the quail could not be
happier to be brown-grey.**

Raccoon

Deep in the tall dark woods
there lived an old raccoon,
Who really wanted
to go on a trip to the moon.

As he had never been
anywhere so far before,
He thought it's his last
opportunity to explore.

He asked all
his flying friends
one by one to go;
Sadly, despite being
convincing,
they all said **"No."**

Finally, his dear old friend
the dragonfly
Agreed to take him to
the deep blue starry sky.

So off they went together
to visit the full moon
Just as the sun was setting
in the late afternoon.

The iridescent dragonfly
flew with all his might
And they reached the bright moon
in the middle of the night.

What an amazing
journey it had been!
So full of memories
of lovely things they'd seen.

Snake

In bygone times when
giraffes' necks were not long at all
A snake lay curled up on a tree
that was rather tall.

Looking down casually
at the murky swamp below,
He noticed one of those
short-necked giraffes walking slow.

The giraffe stretched to reach
a tasty leaf hanging down,
When she lost balance in the bog
and began to drown.

In despair, she tried to hold on
to surrounding grass,
But it was too weak to hold
the giraffe's heavy mass.

In response to the sinking
giraffe's desperate yelp,
The snake instantly lowered down
to offer his help.

He clenched his wide mouth
round her neck and began to pull,
But she was badly stuck
with her body immersed in full.

The long snake tensed his body
and pulled with all his strength;
While the giraffe's neck kept
stretching in length!

Snap! With the snake's help
the giraffe flew out of the swamp;
Excited with her new long neck
she would sing and romp.

Gifted with long necks
ever since that day,
Giraffes can pluck
the highest leaves
as they jump and play.

Tiger

In a distant tropical jungle so wild and dense,
Lived a large tiger who every morning woke up tense.

Why with colourful plants surrounding him
were his dreams just black and white?
It was rather grim.

**"Every day I go to bed
in a fantastic mood,
But in the morning, I wake
up quite cranky and rude!"**

"What could be happening
to me when I go to bed?"

The puzzled tiger
thought long and hard,
scratching his head.

One day he lay down
and pretended
he was sleeping,

When just over his head
he saw a spider creeping.

The spider lowered down
on his web ever so vast,
Trying to catch the colourful dreams
as they flew past.

He would then weave them
into the **most amazing thread**
And his already large spider web
would spread and spread.

That’s why his dreams
were black and white,
there’s nothing more to say.
The tiger roared and leapt
and chased the thief away.

Umbrellabird

In a dense tropical forest
where rain didn't stop
Stood a family of ladybugs
trapped in a drop.

With their wings soaking wet
they simply couldn't fly,
So they waited patiently
for the rain to pass by.

Suddenly, a big shadow
appeared on the drenched ground
And the air was filled with
a loud squeaky sound.

An inky umbrellabird landed in a puddle,
Offering to rescue the insects from this muddle.

Just above his pointed beak
an impressive crest spread
Like a dry umbrella shelter
right above his head.

Thrilled, the ladybugs
climbed on the bird's
beak one by one,
Really looking forward
to drying in the hot sun.

The umbrellabird
took off swiftly
from the storm,
Reaching a dense leafy
tree branch that was
dry and warm.

He hovered over the leaves
with his feathers so sleek,
Whilst the grateful ladybugs
disembarked from his beak.

Then they all marched up
the tree branch in an orderly line,
To watch the streaking rays
of yellow sunshine.

Vulture

In a high mountain range
covered in piles of fresh snow
Lived a lonely vulture where
strong northern winds would blow.

Flying one morning through
fluffy clouds and blue sky
He saw a tasty looking
carcass lying nearby.

What could be more delicious than a meaty white bone?
The vulture thought
he could have it all
on his own.

He then landed
on a cliff next to
the crunchy treat
And grabbing it
with his beak
began to eat.

The vulture swallowed
the piece of bone
all in one bite,
But it felt too heavy
and just didn't feel right.

It got stuck in his throat
and wouldn't go in or out.
The vulture tried
to get help but
couldn't even shout.

He struggled to breathe
and turned sickly blue.

He thought, "**What is going on, am I getting bird flu?**"

From nowhere a mountain lion jumped down with his bunch
And saved the vulture by giving him a strong belly punch.

The vulture coughed and out of his beak came a **large stone**
That he had mistaken for a crunchy piece of bone!

Worm

Deep under the dry surface
of the fragrant grassy plain
Lived a long worm,
impatiently waiting for some rain;

For that moment when
the water soaks up the dry soil,
So he can lie in a puddle,
relax and uncoil.

Next morning a torrential
downpour filled up the sky;
The dry earth got soaked well
and was no longer so dry.

Instantly, the worm came out
of his underground home
In search of a large puddle
in between the wet loam.

But when he got
to a puddle and looked down,
He saw another worm
looking at him with a frown!

The worm wriggled to
the next puddle
to look inside,

But there
another one
looked back with
eyes open wide!

They were all mocking him,
which he found extremely rude
And the situation put
the worm in a very bad mood.

Suddenly, a strong gust of wind rushed through the puddle,
Shaking the water and creating a big muddle.

Just like that the wind made
all the rude worms disappear.
The stunned worm thought
**they must have all
hidden out of fear!**

He quickly took the opportunity to dive in
And lay content in the murky puddle with a wide grin.

Xerus

A tiny xerus lived
in a deserted grassland
Surrounded by not much
apart from the loam
and sand.

The sky turned dark and
he felt a raindrop on his nose;
He wanted to look for food
before the waters rose.

But the hungry xerus failed
to find a single bite to eat;
He got so tired he
couldn't stand on his feet.

The dark clouds kept on coming
and the rain wouldn't stop.
All hope was lost to find food
and he felt like a flop.

He lay on his back when
the sweetest scent
filled his snoot;
Ah! On the other bank
he spotted a juicy fruit.

With no means of getting across,
since he couldn't swim,
The chances of filling his belly
looked rather slim.

He sighed, **"I am soaking wet
and hungry. I give up!"**
Then suddenly the rain stopped
and a rainbow came up.

"A colourful bridge!
I can't believe my luck!" he cried,
He climbed the rainbow
and slid down to the other side.

Xerus grabbed the lush fruit
and had it all in one go.
This was an opportunity
he simply couldn't blow!

Yak

On cold snowy slopes
of the highest peak in the world
Lived a large herd of wild yaks
with their long fringes curled.

As the weather was
terribly bad up high,
The yaks all agreed
to look for shelter nearby.

A freezing wind started to blow
and confused the smallest yak
Who lost the others
and slowly fell back.

While the others walked down
the icy slope to a safe haven,
The small yak got discovered
by an inky raven.

"Are you lost?" asked the raven
concerned for the yak's sake.

**"To find your herd,
take a shortcut through
this frozen lake."**

"I don't know how to skate,"
said the yak with concern,

**"How to keep my balance,
stop or even make a turn."**

"I'll teach you!" said the raven
nesting in the yak's fringe.
The yak stepped on the slippery ice
that made him cringe.

He caught his balance and made
the most amazing spin;
He was so proud that his face
filled with a big grin.

Then together they skated
across the frozen rink
And they both made it
to the other side in a blink.

Zz

Zebra

Right in the middle
of a vicious thunderstorm
Bounced a little zebra,
looking at black clouds form;

Playing, not worried about
the weather being rough,
Not scared of the lightning,
she thought she was
so tough.

The animals warned her
not to play under the tree,
But the zebra kept
bouncing around
the big trunk in glee.

Suddenly, the bright lightning
struck right onto her tail.
The terrified zebra froze
and became really pale.

Her tail caught fire
and flames burned bright and red;
The zebra jumped up
and away from the tree she fled.

But that didn't stop the blaze from growing higher.
The zebra screamed: **"Please help me put out the fire!"**

Then, the ground shook and the air got thick with dust,
As an elephant ran to her blowing a mighty gust.

He sucked water from a puddle
until the level sunk,
Then put out the fire
by spraying it through his trunk.

Kinga White is a Polish born award-winning graphic designer and illustrator. She studied English Language Teaching at the University of Warsaw, Design and Fine Art at the College of Fine Art and Graphic Design in Poland as well as Graphic Design at the London Metropolitan University, U.K.

Since graduating she has worked in publishing, international commercial businesses as well as government bodies in the U.K. and abroad.

She now lives in the suburbs of London with her husband and two boys.

Animalphabetical Adventures is a marriage of her two passions: education and art. In this debut book she has combined language teaching through story telling with her illustrations to support and inspire children on their path to reading fluency.

www.kingawhite.com

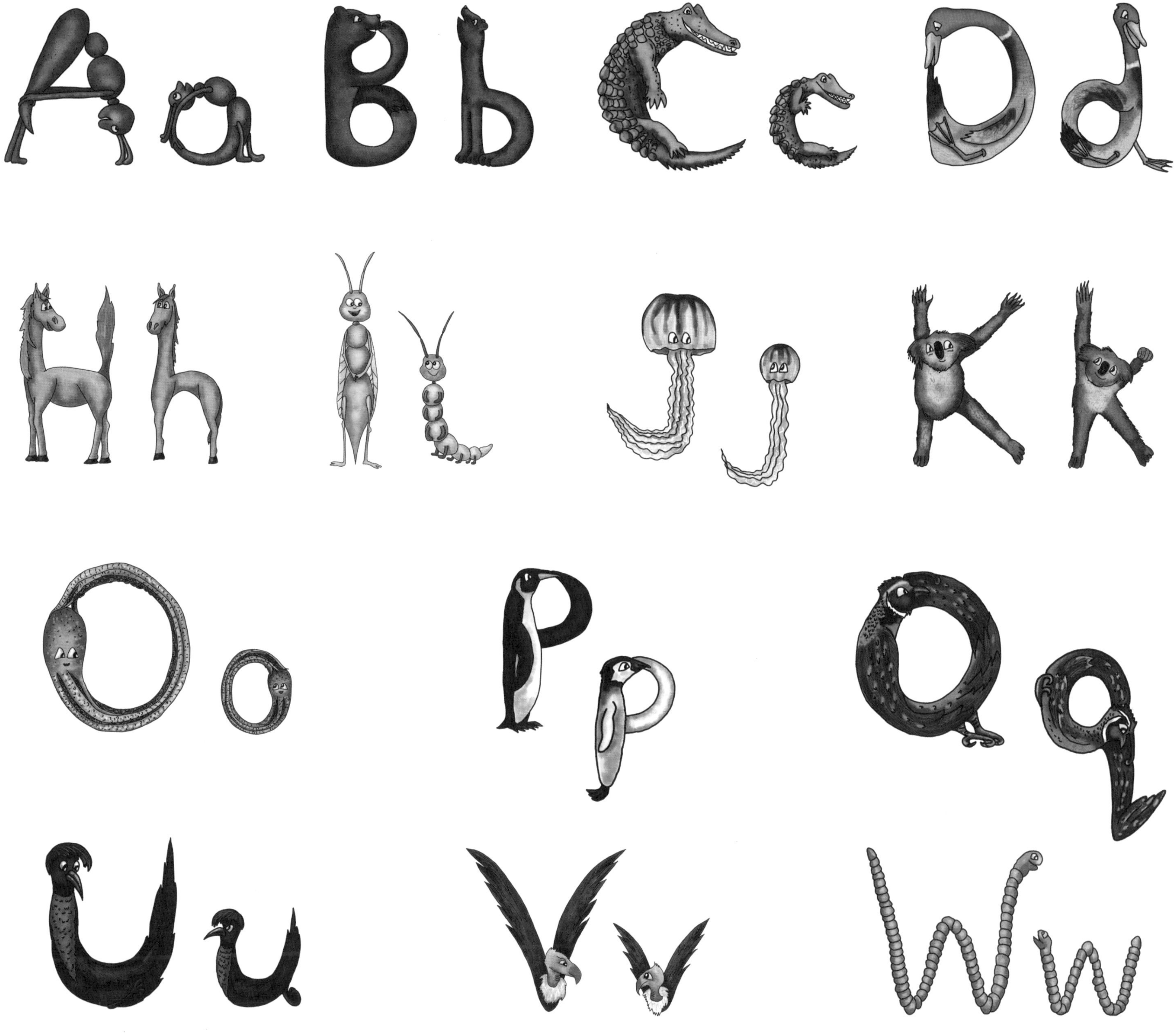

Aa Bb Cc Dd

Hh Ii Jj Kk

Oo Pp Qq

Uu Vv Ww